I060025б

# THE SUNFLOWER CENTER

Rene' Stanley

Books By Rene'

Cover Design by Rene' Stanley

ISBN: 979-8-9997823-0-4 (paperback)

Library of Congress Control Number: 2025903504

bbr@renes-books.us

https://booksbyrene.com

1 edition 2025

# CONTENTS

# PREFACE

This is a story about grief. But more than that, it's a story about what grows after grief – the unexpected blooms that can emerge from the most desolate of landscapes. It's a story about the enduring power of human connection, the surprising resilience of the spirit, and the trans-formative magic of art.

I didn't set out to write a story about loss. I started with a chipped ceramic mug, a trembling hand, and the phantom scent of blood. The character of Imani emerged from there, a woman haunted by a tragedy that had irrevocably altered her life. As I wrote, I discovered that her story wasn't just about surviving; it was about finding a way to thrive, to create meaning and beauty from the broken pieces.

Kayla, Imani's best friend, became the sunflower – a symbol of light, joy, and a life cut short. Her memory became the catalyst for Imani's journey, a guiding force that propelled her forward, even when the darkness threatened to overwhelm her.

The Sunflower Center, the heart of this story, is a fictional creation, but it's inspired by the very real power of art therapy and the profound impact of community support. I've witnessed firsthand the way creative expression can unlock emotions, facilitate healing, and foster connections that transcend words. This story is a tribute to that power, a celebration of the human capacity to find hope and resilience in the face of unimaginable loss.

This is not a story with a neat and tidy ending. Grief doesn't work that way. It's a lifelong companion, a constant hum beneath the surface. But it doesn't have to define us. It can be a part of our story, a catalyst for growth, a source of empathy, and a reminder of the preciousness of life.

This is Imani's story. It's Kayla's story. And in a way, it's a story for all of us who have navigated loss, who have sought solace in creativity, and who have discovered the enduring power of the human spirit to bloom, even in the darkest of gardens.

# Chapter 1

# THE SHATTERED MUG

The chipped ceramic mug warmed Imani's hands, but the tremor remained. It wasn't the cold October air seeping through the cracked windowpane; it was the phantom echo of shattering glass, the metallic tang of blood that still clung to the back of her throat, even two years later. She took a shaky sip of chamomile tea, the floral scent doing little to soothe the jagged edges of her anxiety.

Imani stared out at the bustling city street below her small apartment. People hurried by, heads down, lost in their own worlds, their own worries. She envied their obliviousness. Their ability to walk down a street without flinching at a sudden noise, without scanning every face for a threat that existed only in the fractured landscape of her memory.

\*\*\*

The accident. That's what everyone called it. A drunk driver, a red light ignored, a life irrevocably altered. Imani had survived, physically scarred but alive. Her best friend, Kayla, hadn't. The guilt was a constant, suffocating weight, heavier than any physical burden.

Therapy helped, sometimes. Dr. Lewis, with her kind eyes and gentle probing, had given Imani tools: breathing exercises, grounding techniques, the mantra "I am safe. I am here. I am present." But the tools felt flimsy, like trying to patch a dam with a band-aid.

Tonight was particularly bad. The anniversary loomed, a dark cloud on the horizon. Imani knew she should call her mom, hear the familiar, comforting cadence of her voice. But the words caught in her throat, choked by the fear of burdening her mother with the same pain that consumed her.

She closed her eyes, trying to conjure Kayla's face, the way her smile could light up a room, the way her laughter used to bubble up like a joyful spring. But the image was fragmented, distorted by the horror of that night. The screech of tires, the blinding headlights, the sickening crunch of metal...

A sudden car horn blared from the street below, and Imani jumped, the mug slipping from her grasp and shattering on the floor. The sound, so similar to the one that haunted her nightmares, ripped through her carefully constructed defenses. She crumpled to the floor, her body wracked with sobs, the shards of ceramic mirroring the broken pieces of her heart.

The tears came, hot and heavy, a release she hadn't allowed herself in weeks. She cried for Kayla, for the future they had lost, for the carefree girl she used to be. She cried for the fear that clung to her like a second skin, for the constant battle to just...breathe.

As the sobs subsided, a flicker of something else emerged. Not hope, not yet. But a tiny spark of defiance. A refusal to let the darkness win. She was still here. She was still breathing. And maybe, just maybe, that was enough for now.

Slowly, painstakingly, Imani picked up the pieces of the broken mug. Her hands still trembled, but there was a new steadiness in her gaze. She would clean up the mess. She would face the anniversary. She would keep fighting. Not because she was strong, but because she had to. For Kayla. For herself. For the fragile, flickering possibility of a future where the echoes didn't scream quite so loud.

The scent of chamomile and spilled tea mingled with the lingering, metallic ghost-scent that always seemed to accompany her panic attacks. Imani wrapped her arms around herself, the thin cotton of her pajamas offering little protection against the chill that had settled deep in her bones. She stayed there on the floor, amidst the shattered ceramic, for a long time, letting the quiet hum of the city filter through the window, a grounding counterpoint to the chaos within.

Finally, the shaking subsided enough for her to push herself up. Her knees ached, a dull reminder of the physical scars that crisscrossed her body, permanent etchings of that night. She carefully swept up the broken pieces of the mug, the sharp edges a tangible representation of the invisible wounds she carried.

As she worked, her phone buzzed on the counter. She glanced at the screen: a text from her mom. "Thinking of you, baby girl. Call me when you can. "

Imani's chest tightened. Her mother's love was a lifeline, a constant source of warmth, but it also came with a heavy dose of guilt. She knew her mother worried, carried the weight of Imani's pain alongside her own. The urge to isolate, to protect her mother from the darkness, was strong. But tonight, something shifted. The spark of defiance that had flickered earlier grew a little brighter.

She picked up the phone and dialed. Her mother answered on the second ring, her voice laced with concern.

"Imani? Honey, are you okay?"

"Not really, Mom," Imani admitted, her voice trembling. "It's... it's been a rough night."

She didn't go into details, not yet. But she let her mother's voice wash over her, the familiar cadence soothing the raw edges of her anxiety. They talked about small things – the weather, a funny story about Imani's niece, the upcoming family dinner.

"Are you coming to dinner on Sunday, Imani?" her mother asked, a hopeful note in her voice.

Imani hesitated. Large gatherings were usually a minefield. Too many people, too much noise, too many potential triggers. But the thought of being surrounded by family, by their unwavering love and support, held a surprising appeal.

"I... I think so, Mom," Imani said, the words feeling surprisingly firm. "I'll try."

"That's all I ask, baby girl," her mother said softly. "Just try."

After they hung up, Imani felt a shift. The weight hadn't vanished, but it felt... lighter. Talking to her mother, making the decision to face the upcoming family gathering, had given her a small sense of agency, a feeling that she wasn't entirely at the mercy of her PTSD.

She went back to the window, looking out at the city lights. The fear was still there, a constant hum beneath the surface, but it no longer felt all-consuming. She knew the road ahead would be long and winding, filled with setbacks and moments of overwhelming darkness. But she also knew she wasn't alone. She had her therapist, her mother, her family. And she had that tiny, flickering spark of defiance, the stubborn refusal to let the past define her future.

She took a deep breath, the cold air filling her lungs. It was a start. A shaky, fragile, but undeniable start. And for tonight, that was enough.

# Chapter 2

# THE
# ANNIVERSARY

The next few days were a blur of restless nights and anxious days. Imani went through the motions of her life – work at the small bookstore, therapy sessions with Dr. Lewis, solitary meals in her apartment – but the looming anniversary cast a long shadow over everything.

Dr. Lewis had encouraged her to create a ritual, something to honor Kayla's memory and acknowledge the grief that threatened to consume her. Imani resisted at first. Rituals felt... forced. Like trying to contain a tidal wave with a teacup. But the alternative – sinking back into the suffocating darkness – was even less appealing.

So, she decided on a small act of remembrance. Kayla had loved sunflowers, their bright, sunny faces a stark contrast to the darkness that had surrounded their final moments together. Imani bought a single sunflower, its head heavy with golden petals, and placed it on her windowsill.

The flower, a vibrant splash of color against the grey cityscape, became a focal point. A reminder of Kayla's light, and a silent promise to keep fighting for her own.

The day of the anniversary dawned cold and grey, mirroring the turmoil in Imani's chest. She woke with a knot of anxiety in her stomach, the phantom metallic tang back in her throat. The breathing exercises, the grounding techniques, felt useless.

She almost called her mom to cancel the family dinner. The thought of facing the well-meaning but potentially overwhelming condolences, the pitying glances, was almost unbearable. But the image of the sunflower, bathed in the weak morning light, stopped her.

She would go. Not because she felt strong, but because she had promised. And because, deep down, a tiny part of her craved the comfort of connection, the warmth of family.

The bus ride to her parents' house was a sensory overload. The rumble of the engine, the screech of brakes, the chatter of other passengers – each sound grated on her frayed nerves. She closed her eyes, focusing on the steady rhythm of her breathing, trying to block out the external chaos.

When she arrived, the house was filled with the familiar aroma of her mother's cooking, a comforting blend of spices and roasted vegetables. Her niece, Maya, a whirlwind of five-year-old energy, greeted her with a gap-toothed grin and a hug that nearly knocked the wind out of her.

"Auntie Imani! You came!"

Imani managed a smile, the warmth of Maya's embrace momentarily easing the tension in her shoulders. "Of course, I came, sweetie."

The dinner itself was a mixture of comfort and quiet pain. Her family tiptoed around the subject of the anniversary, their eyes filled with a mixture of love and unspoken grief. Imani appreciated their efforts, but the unspoken weight in the room was almost as heavy as direct condolences would have been.

After dinner, as the family gathered in the living room, Imani's mother pulled her aside. "Honey, are you alright?" she asked softly, her hand resting on Imani's arm.

Imani hesitated, then nodded. "I'm... managing," she said, the words feeling both true and inadequate.

Her mother studied her face, her eyes filled with a depth of understanding that only a mother could possess. "Kayla would be so proud of you, you know," she said quietly. "She'd want you to live, Imani. To really live."

The words, spoken with such gentle conviction, struck a chord deep within Imani. They weren't a magic cure, but they were a reminder. A reminder of the life Kayla had lost, and the responsibility Imani felt to honor that life by embracing her own.

The spark of defiance, which had flickered so faintly in the preceding days, began to burn a little brighter. It was a small flame, vulnerable to the winds of grief and fear, but it was there. And it was growing.

Imani took a deep breath, the scent of her mother's lavender-infused hand cream a familiar comfort. "I know, Mom," she whispered, her voice thick with emotion. "It's just... hard."

Her mother squeezed her arm. "I know it is, baby. But you're stronger than you think."

They stood in silence for a moment, the sounds of laughter and conversation from the living room washing over them. Imani felt a wave of gratitude for her family, for their unwavering love and support. It was a lifeline, a constant source of strength in the turbulent sea of her grief.

Later, as Maya played with her toys on the floor, Imani found herself drawn to the family photo album. She hadn't looked at it in years, the memories it held too painful to confront. But tonight, something compelled her to open it.

The first few pages were filled with pictures of her and Kayla as children. Silly faces, awkward poses, the undeniable evidence of a bond that had stretched back to their earliest memories. Imani traced the outline of Kayla's smiling face in one photo, a pang of loss so sharp it almost took her breath away.

But as she turned the pages, she found something else. Pictures of Kayla with her family, with other friends, living a life that extended beyond their shared experiences. Pictures of Kayla laughing, dancing, celebrating. Pictures that captured the essence of her vibrant spirit, the joy that had radiated from her like sunshine.

And then, a picture of Imani, taken a few months after the accident. She was standing by Kayla's grave, her face pale and drawn, her eyes hollow with grief. But there was something else in the photo, something she hadn't noticed before. A faint glimmer of determination in her gaze, a subtle set to her jaw that spoke of resilience.

It was a reminder. A reminder that she had survived. That she had continued to live, to fight, even when the darkness threatened to consume her. And that, she realized, was a testament to Kayla's spirit as much as anything else.

As she closed the album, a sense of peace settled over her. It wasn't a complete absence of pain, but a quiet acceptance. The grief was still there, a constant companion, but it no longer felt like a crushing weight. It was a part of her, woven into the fabric of her being, but it didn't define her.

The next day, Imani went back to the bookstore. The familiar scent of old paper and leather, the quiet hum of turning pages, soothed her frayed nerves. She found a small, empty space on a shelf and placed a framed picture of Kayla there, a smiling image from their high school graduation.

It was a small gesture, but it felt significant. A way of keeping Kayla's memory alive, not just in her heart, but in the world around her. A way of acknowledging the impact she had had on her life, and the enduring power of their friendship.

As she stepped back to admire the photo, a customer approached her. "Excuse me," he said, "I'm looking for a book on coping with grief."

Imani met his gaze, her eyes filled with a quiet understanding. She knew that journey. She was still walking it.

"I think I can help you with that," she said, a small, genuine smile gracing her lips. And in that moment, she knew that she wasn't just helping him. She was helping herself. She was continuing to heal, to grow, to find a way to live with the echoes, and to honor the memory of the friend who had taught her the true meaning of resilience. The sunflower was still on her windowsill, and though starting to wilt, continued to remind her of her promise.

## Chapter 3

# FINDING COLOR

The weeks following the anniversary passed in a slow, steady rhythm. The sharp edges of Imani's grief began to soften, replaced by a dull ache that was almost... bearable. She found herself engaging more fully in her life, rediscovering small joys she had forgotten existed. The smell of freshly brewed coffee in the morning, the crisp autumn air on her face during her walks to work, the quiet satisfaction of recommending the perfect book to a customer.

Work at the bookstore became a sanctuary. The hushed atmosphere, the weight of countless stories in her hands, the connection with people seeking solace and escape in the pages of a book – it all provided a sense of grounding, a connection to something larger than herself. She started a small "In Memoriam" shelf, featuring books about grief, loss, and resilience, alongside the picture of

Kayla. It became a quiet corner of the store, a space for reflection and shared understanding.

One rainy afternoon, a young woman with tear-stained eyes approached the shelf. She hovered hesitantly, her fingers tracing the spines of the books. Imani recognized the raw, fragile look in her eyes, the echo of her own pain.

"Can I help you find something?" Imani asked gently.

The woman looked up, startled. "I... I don't even know where to start," she whispered, her voice choked with emotion. "My brother... he died last week. It was... sudden."

Imani's heart ached in sympathy. She knew that feeling, the disorientation, the overwhelming sense of loss that threatened to swallow you whole. "I'm so sorry," she said softly. "It's... the hardest thing."

She guided the woman through the books on the shelf, sharing her own experiences, offering words of comfort and understanding. They talked for a long time, a shared connection forged in the crucible of grief. As the woman left, clutching a book on healing after loss, she turned to Imani with a grateful smile.

"Thank you," she said, her voice still trembling but filled with a newfound strength. "You... you really helped."

Imani watched her go, a warmth spreading through her chest. It wasn't a cure, not for either of them. But it was a connection, a reminder that they weren't alone in their pain. And that, she realized, was a powerful thing.

Dr. Lewis noticed the change in Imani during their sessions. Her eyes were brighter, her posture more upright, her voice filled with a newfound confidence. "You seem... lighter," Dr. Lewis observed.

Imani smiled, a genuine smile that reached her eyes. "I am," she said. "It's still hard, of course. The grief is always there. But it's... different. It doesn't feel like it's going to consume me anymore."

They talked about the "In Memoriam" shelf, about the connection she had made with the young woman, about the small steps she was taking to reclaim her life. Dr. Lewis nodded, her eyes filled with approval.

"You're finding your way, Imani," she said. "You're honoring Kayla's memory by living your own life, by finding meaning and connection in the midst of your grief. That's... powerful."

The conversation with Dr. Lewis solidified something within Imani. She was no longer just surviving; she was starting to thrive. The spark of defiance had grown into a steady flame, fueled by her connection to others, by her commitment to honoring Kayla's memory, and by her own growing resilience.

One evening, as she was walking home from work, she passed a small art studio. The window displayed a collection of vibrant paintings, bursts of color that drew her in. She had always loved art, had even dabbled in painting herself before the accident. But the fear of revisiting that part of herself, the fear of unlocking the emotions she had kept carefully contained, had kept her away.

Tonight, however, something shifted. The colors called to her, a siren song of creativity and expression. She hesitated for a moment, then pushed open the door.

The studio was filled with the scent of paint and turpentine, the air buzzing with a quiet energy. A woman with kind eyes and paint-splattered overalls greeted her.

"Welcome," she said. "Are you interested in a class?"

Imani's heart pounded in her chest. The fear was still there, a familiar tremor in her hands. But the desire to create, to express herself, to reconnect with that lost part of herself, was stronger.

"I... I think so," she said, her voice barely a whisper.

The woman smiled. "Wonderful. We have a beginner's class starting next week. It's a safe space, a place to explore and express yourself without judgment."

Imani took a deep breath, the scent of paint filling her lungs. It felt like coming home.

"I'll sign up," she said, the words firm and clear.

As she walked home, the city lights seemed brighter, the air crisper. She was still afraid, still grieving, still carrying the echoes of the past. But she was also hopeful, excited, and filled with a newfound sense of purpose. She was taking another step, a small but significant step, on the long and winding road to healing. And she knew, with a certainty that settled deep in her bones, that she wasn't alone. She had Kayla's memory, her family's love, and her own growing strength to guide her. And that, she realized, was more than enough. It was everything.

The beginner's art class was held in a sun-drenched room above the studio, the walls lined with shelves overflowing with tubes of paint, brushes of every size, and canvases in various stages of completion. The air hummed with a quiet, creative energy, a stark contrast to the sterile environment of Dr. Lewis's office, yet somehow just as therapeutic.

There were five other students in the class, a diverse group ranging in age and experience. A shy teenager with bright pink hair, a retired gentleman with a neatly trimmed beard, a middle-aged woman with a warm smile, and a young couple who held hands throughout the instructor's introduction. Imani felt a flicker of anxiety, the familiar fear of being an outsider, of not belonging. But the instructor, whose name was Sarah, had a calming presence, her voice soothing and encouraging.

"This is a space for exploration," Sarah said, her eyes sweeping across the room. "There are no mistakes here, only opportunities to learn and grow. Don't be afraid to experiment, to get messy, to let your emotions flow onto the canvas."

Imani took a deep breath, the scent of linseed oil and acrylics a strange comfort. She had brought a small, blank canvas and a set of basic paints, a hesitant offering to the creative spirit she had long suppressed. As Sarah demonstrated basic techniques – mixing colors, applying brushstrokes, creating texture – Imani found herself drawn in, her initial apprehension slowly fading.

When it was time to paint, however, the fear returned. Her hand trembled as she picked up a brush, the blank canvas a daunting expanse of white. She glanced around the room, watching the other students confidently applying paint to their canvases, their faces illuminated by a mixture of concentration and joy.

Doubt gnawed at her. What if she couldn't do it? What if the emotions that poured out were too raw, too overwhelming? What if the darkness consumed her again?

Then, she remembered Kayla. Remembered her infectious laughter, her unwavering belief in Imani's talent, her encouragement to always embrace creativity. She thought of the sunflower, now a dried, brittle reminder of light and resilience, sitting on her windowsill.

Taking a deep breath, Imani dipped her brush into a vibrant yellow, the color of sunflowers, the color of hope. She hesitated for a moment, then made a tentative stroke on the canvas. It wasn't perfect, not by any means. But it was a start.

Slowly, painstakingly, she began to paint. She didn't have a plan, no specific image in mind. She simply let the colors flow, letting her emotions guide her brushstrokes. Yellows blended into oranges, then into reds, a fiery sunset of grief and anger. Then, a touch of blue, the color of tears, the color of sadness. And finally, a hint of green, the color of growth, the color of new beginnings.

As she painted, the tension in her body began to ease. The fear didn't disappear entirely, but it receded, replaced by a sense of focus, of immersion in the creative process. The world outside the studio faded away, the only reality the canvas in front of her, the colors swirling and blending, the emotions finding a voice.

Hours passed in what felt like minutes. Imani lost track of time, lost in the act of creation. When Sarah announced that the class was over, she was surprised to find that her canvas was filled, a vibrant tapestry of colors and textures, a visual representation of her journey through grief.

It wasn't a masterpiece, not in the traditional sense. But it was hers. It was honest, raw, and deeply personal. And as she looked at it, she felt a sense of accomplishment, a quiet pride in what she had created.

The other students gathered around, offering words of encouragement and appreciation. The pink-haired teenager smiled shyly. "I love the colors," she said. "It's... intense."

The retired gentleman nodded. "It has a real energy to it," he added.

The middle-aged woman smiled warmly. "It's beautiful," she said. "It tells a story."

Imani felt a warmth spread through her chest, a sense of connection with these strangers, a shared understanding forged in the crucible of creativity. It wasn't just about the painting; it was about the willingness to be vulnerable, to express emotions, to connect with others on a deeper level.

As she packed up her supplies, Sarah approached her. "That was wonderful, Imani," she said, her eyes filled with genuine appreciation. "You have a real gift."

Imani blushed, her cheeks flushed with a mixture of embarrassment and pride. "Thank you," she said. "It... it felt good."

"Keep painting," Sarah encouraged. "Don't let that fire go out."

Imani nodded, her heart filled with a newfound determination. She would keep painting. She would continue to explore this rediscovered part of herself, to use art as a tool for healing, for expression, for connection.

She walked home that night, the city lights twinkling around her like a million tiny stars. The fear was still there, a subtle hum beneath the surface, but it no longer felt overwhelming. She had found a new outlet, a new way to navigate the complex landscape of her grief. And as she looked up at the night sky, she felt a sense of hope, a quiet confidence that she was on the right path. The path to healing. The path to rediscovering herself. The path to honoring Kayla's memory by living her own life, fully and vibrantly, with all its colors and textures, its shadows and light. The sunflower, though brittle, had done its job, and a new bud of courage, painted on canvas, had begun to bloom.

# Chapter 4

# THE ART OF CONNECTION

The art class became a weekly ritual, a sanctuary where Imani could shed the weight of her grief and immerse herself in the vibrant world of color and texture. It wasn't just about the painting; it was about the community she found there, the shared vulnerability, the unspoken understanding that transcended words.

The pink-haired teenager, whose name was Chloe, became a surprising friend. Initially reserved and hesitant, Chloe gradually opened up, sharing her own struggles with anxiety and depression. They found solace in each other's company, a bond forged in the shared language of art and the quiet understanding of navigating mental health challenges.

One evening, after class, Chloe confided in Imani. "I... I used to cut myself," she whispered, her voice barely audible. "It was the only way I could feel... anything. But the art... it's different. It's like... I can pour all those feelings onto the canvas instead of into my skin."

Imani's heart ached for Chloe, recognizing the familiar desperation, the need to find an outlet for overwhelming emotions. She shared her own experiences, the phantom metallic tang, the constant fear, the way art had become a lifeline.

"It's not a cure," Imani said, her voice gentle. "But it's a way to cope. A way to express what words can't."

They walked home together that night, the city lights blurring into a kaleidoscope of color. The silence between them wasn't awkward; it was filled with a shared understanding, a silent promise of support.

The retired gentleman, Mr. Henderson, was another unexpected source of comfort. He had lost his wife a few years earlier, and the art class was his way of reconnecting with the world, of finding joy in the midst of his grief. He had a gentle wisdom, a quiet strength that Imani found inspiring.

"Grief is like the ocean," he said one evening, as they were cleaning their brushes. "It comes in waves. Sometimes it's calm, barely a ripple. Other times, it's a storm that threatens to drown you. But the waves always recede. And eventually, you learn to swim."

His words resonated deeply with Imani. She was learning to swim. She was learning to navigate the turbulent waters of her grief, to find moments of peace and joy amidst the storm.

The middle-aged woman, Sarah (not the instructor), had a contagious laugh and a warm, maternal presence. She had experienced her own share of loss, but she radiated a resilience that Imani admired. She often brought homemade cookies to class, a small gesture of kindness that filled the room with warmth.

The young couple, always holding hands, painted collaborative pieces, their canvases merging into a single expression of shared love and creativity. They were a reminder of the power of connection, of the beauty of finding solace in another person.

Imani continued to paint, her canvases evolving from abstract expressions of grief to more representational pieces. She painted sunflowers, of course, vibrant tributes to Kayla's memory. But she also painted cityscapes, portraits of her new friends, and even a whimsical self-portrait, her face illuminated by a mischievous grin.

One evening, as she was working on a painting of Chloe, capturing the delicate curve of her cheek, the vibrant pink of her hair, she realized something profound. She wasn't just painting Chloe; she was painting herself. She was capturing the beauty, the resilience, the strength that she saw in her friend, and in doing so, she was recognizing those qualities within herself.

The art wasn't just an outlet; it was a mirror. A reflection of her own healing, her own growth, her own journey towards self-acceptance.

As the weeks passed, Imani found herself feeling more confident, more grounded, more... whole. The fear hadn't vanished entirely, but it no longer controlled her. She was learning to live with the echoes, to find beauty in the midst of the pain, to embrace the messy, imperfect tapestry of her life.

One day, she received a text from her mother. "Family dinner on Sunday? Maya's been asking about you."

Imani smiled. She hadn't missed a family dinner since the anniversary. The gatherings were no longer a minefield; they were a source of comfort, a reminder of the unwavering love and support that surrounded her.

"I'll be there," she texted back.

She arrived at her parents' house to the familiar aroma of her mother's cooking, the sound of Maya's laughter echoing through the rooms. She was greeted with hugs, smiles, and a warmth that settled deep in her bones.

During dinner, Maya, perched on Imani's lap, pointed to a painting hanging on the wall. It was an old landscape, a piece Imani had painted years ago, before the accident.

"Auntie Imani, did you paint that?" Maya asked, her eyes wide with wonder.

Imani smiled. "I did," she said. "A long time ago."

"It's beautiful," Maya said, her voice filled with genuine admiration. "Can you teach me to paint?"

Imani's heart swelled with emotion. It was a full-circle moment, a reminder of the healing power of art, the way it could connect generations, bridge the gap between past and present.

"Of course, I can," Imani said, her voice filled with love. "We can start tomorrow."

After dinner, as the family gathered in the living room, Imani's mother pulled her aside. "You seem... different, honey," she said, her eyes searching Imani's face. "Happier."

Imani nodded. "I am," she said. "I'm... finding my way."

Her mother smiled, her eyes filled with a mixture of pride and relief. "I'm so proud of you, Imani," she said. "You've come so far."

Imani knew she still had a long way to go. The journey of healing was a lifelong process, filled with ups and downs, setbacks and triumphs. But she also knew that she was no longer alone. She had her family, her friends, her art, and her own growing strength to guide her.

As she looked around the room, at the faces of the people she loved, she felt a sense of gratitude, a deep appreciation for the connections that sustained her. She was still grieving, still carrying the echoes of the past. But she was also living, loving, creating, and finding her way back to herself.

And as she looked at the old landscape painting, a reminder of the artist she had been, and the artist she was becoming, she knew that she was on the right path. The path to healing, to wholeness, to a future where the echoes didn't scream quite so loud, where the colors were vibrant, and where the sunflowers always bloomed. She smiled, a genuine smile from somewhere deep inside, somewhere untouched by tragedy, and knew she was finally home. The sunflower, though long gone, had scattered seeds she hadn't noticed, and now, they had finally taken root.

The following weeks unfolded like a time-lapse photograph of a blossoming flower. Imani's life, once muted and confined, began to burst with color and texture, much like the canvases she filled with increasing confidence. The art class was no longer just a refuge; it was a catalyst.

One crisp Saturday morning, Sarah, the instructor, announced a small, local art exhibition. "It's a chance to showcase your work," she said, her eyes twinkling. "Nothing fancy, just a community event. Anyone interested?"

Imani's heart leaped, a mixture of excitement and terror churning in her stomach. The thought of displaying her art, of exposing her vulnerability to the world, was daunting. But the idea of sharing her journey, of perhaps connecting with others through her work, was also incredibly compelling.

Chloe, her pink hair even brighter than usual, nudged her. "You should do it, Imani," she said, her voice filled with genuine enthusiasm. "Your work is amazing."

Mr. Henderson, ever the voice of quiet encouragement, added, "It's a wonderful opportunity, Imani. Don't let fear hold you back."

Sarah, seeing Imani's hesitation, smiled gently. "It's not about judgment, Imani," she said. "It's about sharing your voice, your story. And your story is worth telling."

Imani looked at the faces of her friends, their support a tangible force. She thought of Kayla, of the sunflower, of the journey she had taken. She thought of the young woman in the bookstore, the connection they had shared, the power of art to heal and connect.

"Okay," she said, her voice trembling slightly, but filled with a newfound resolve. "I'll do it."

The decision ignited a spark within her. She spent the next few weeks immersed in preparation, selecting the pieces she wanted to display, carefully framing them, writing short descriptions that captured the essence of each work. She chose the abstract piece from her first class, the fiery sunset of grief and hope. She chose the portrait of Chloe, a vibrant testament to resilience and friendship. And she chose a new piece, a large canvas filled with sunflowers, their golden heads reaching towards the sky, a tribute to Kayla and a celebration of life.

The day of the exhibition dawned bright and clear, a perfect autumn day. Imani arrived at the community center, her heart pounding in her chest, her hands clammy with nerves. The room was buzzing with activity, artists setting up their displays, visitors milling around, the air filled with a mixture of anticipation and excitement.

Chloe and Mr. Henderson were there, offering words of encouragement and helping her arrange her display. Sarah (the classmate), beaming with pride, brought a bouquet of sunflowers, a thoughtful gesture that brought tears to Imani's eyes. Even Imani's mother and Maya showed up, Maya bouncing with excitement, her eyes wide with wonder as she looked at Imani's paintings.

As the exhibition opened, Imani felt a wave of vulnerability wash over her. It was one thing to share her art with her friends in the safe space of the art class; it was another to expose it to the scrutiny of strangers. She stood nervously by her display, watching as people approached, their eyes scanning her work, their expressions shifting from curiosity to contemplation to appreciation.

A young couple stopped in front of the sunflower painting, their faces illuminated by a soft glow. "It's beautiful," the woman said, her voice filled with emotion. "It reminds me of my grandmother. She loved sunflowers."

An older man, his eyes filled with a quiet sadness, paused in front of the abstract piece. "It captures the feeling of loss so perfectly," he said, his voice trembling slightly. "The chaos, the pain, but also... the hope."

A teenage girl, her eyes mirroring Chloe's initial shyness, lingered in front of the portrait. "She looks... strong," she said, her voice barely a whisper. "Like she's been through a lot, but she's still standing."

Each comment, each connection, was a balm to Imani's soul. It wasn't about praise or validation; it was about the shared human experience, the way art could transcend words and connect people on a deeper level. It was about the realization that her story, her grief, her resilience, resonated with others, that she wasn't alone in her journey.

As the day wore on, Imani felt a sense of peace settle over her. The fear hadn't vanished entirely, but it had receded, replaced by a quiet confidence, a sense of accomplishment. She had faced her vulnerability, shared her story, and found connection in the process.

Later, as she was packing up her display, a woman approached her. She was the owner of a small, local art gallery. "I've been watching your work all day," she said, her eyes filled with genuine admiration. "I love your style, your use of color, the emotion you convey. I'd be interested in showcasing some of your pieces in my gallery."

Imani was stunned. It was an unexpected opportunity, a validation of her talent, a chance to take her art to a wider audience. She stammered a thank you, her heart soaring with a mixture of excitement and disbelief.

As she walked home that night, the city lights seemed to shimmer with a new brilliance. The echoes of the past were still there, a subtle hum beneath the surface, but they no longer defined her. She had found her voice, her purpose, her connection to the world. She was an artist, a survivor, a friend, a daughter, a woman who had learned to navigate the turbulent waters of grief and emerge stronger, more resilient, more alive.

The sunflower, long gone, had left behind a legacy of beauty, resilience, and hope. And Imani, the girl who had once been shattered by loss, was now blooming, her colors vibrant, her spirit soaring, her heart filled with a quiet, enduring joy. She had found her light, and she was shining brightly.

## Chapter 5

# THE GALLERY SHOWING

The gallery showing felt surreal. Imani had spent weeks preparing, agonizing over which pieces to include, crafting the perfect artist statement, and battling the persistent whispers of self-doubt that threatened to derail her progress. But now, standing in the softly lit space, surrounded by her paintings, a sense of calm washed over her. It wasn't arrogance, not exactly. It was a quiet recognition of how far she'd come, a tangible manifestation of her healing journey.

The gallery owner, Ms. Eleanor Vance, a woman with a keen eye and a warm smile, had been incredibly supportive. She'd chosen a prominent spot for Imani's work, a corner bathed in natural light that showcased the vibrancy of her colors. The sunflower painting, now titled "Kayla's Light," held the central position, a beacon of hope and remembrance.

Chloe, her pink hair now streaked with purple, was there, of course, bouncing with an infectious energy that made Imani smile. Mr. Henderson, looking dapper in a tweed jacket, offered a quiet nod of approval. Sarah (the classmate), her arms laden with another batch of her famous cookies, beamed with pride. Even Dr. Lewis had made an appearance, her kind eyes filled with a warmth that went beyond professional courtesy.

"This is... incredible, Imani," Dr. Lewis said, her voice soft but filled with genuine admiration. "You've taken your pain and transformed it into something beautiful, something that speaks to the human condition. That's... powerful."

Imani felt a lump form in her throat. Dr. Lewis's words, more than any praise from art critics or potential buyers, validated her journey. It was a reminder that her art wasn't just about aesthetics; it was about healing, connection, and resilience.

The opening night was a blur of faces, conversations, and quiet moments of reflection. Imani found herself talking to strangers, sharing the stories behind her paintings, connecting with people on a level she hadn't thought possible. She saw tears in the eyes of a woman who had lost her daughter, a spark of recognition in the gaze of a young man struggling with depression, a quiet nod of understanding from a couple who had navigated their own share of grief.

One interaction stood out. A young woman, her face etched with a familiar sadness, lingered in front of "Kayla's Light." She stood there for a long time, her gaze fixed on the vibrant sunflowers, her expression shifting from sorrow to a glimmer of hope.

Imani approached her cautiously. "It's... a tribute to my best friend," she said softly. "She loved sunflowers."

The woman turned, her eyes filled with tears. "My brother," she whispered. "He... he took his own life last year. Sunflowers were his favorite, too."

A wave of empathy washed over Imani. She knew that pain, that raw, gaping hole that loss left behind. She reached out and gently touched the woman's arm. "I'm so sorry," she said. "It's... the hardest thing."

They stood in silence for a moment, a shared understanding passing between them. Then, the woman smiled, a fragile, watery smile, but a smile nonetheless. "Thank you," she said. "For sharing your story. For... for showing me that there's still beauty, even after... after everything."

That moment, more than any sale or critical acclaim, solidified Imani's purpose. Her art wasn't just about her own healing; it was about creating a space for connection, for shared vulnerability, for hope. It was about reminding people that they weren't alone in their pain, that even in the darkest of times, there was still light to be found.

The gallery showing was a success, beyond Imani's wildest dreams. Several of her paintings sold, including the portrait of Chloe, which was purchased by a local art collector. But more importantly, the exhibition sparked conversations, fostered connections, and created a sense of community around the shared experience of grief and resilience.

Ms. Vance was thrilled. "You have a rare gift, Imani," she said, her eyes shining. "You're not just painting; you're touching people's lives. I'd love to represent you, to continue showcasing your work."

Imani was overwhelmed with gratitude. It was an incredible opportunity, a validation of her talent, a chance to pursue her passion on a larger scale. She accepted Ms. Vance's offer, her heart filled with a mixture of excitement and trepidation.

The weeks that followed were a whirlwind of activity. Imani continued to paint, her creativity fueled by the positive response to her work. She experimented with new techniques, explored different themes, but always returned to the core of her artistic voice: the exploration of grief, resilience, and the enduring power of hope.

She also started teaching a small art class at the community center, sharing her knowledge and passion with others who were seeking solace and expression through creativity. She found a deep satisfaction in guiding her students, in witnessing their own journeys of healing and self-discovery.

One of her students was the young woman she had met at the gallery, the one who had lost her brother. Her name was Amelia, and she had a quiet intensity, a raw talent that Imani recognized immediately. They formed a bond, a connection forged in the shared language of art and the unspoken understanding of navigating profound loss.

Imani's life had transformed. She was no longer just surviving; she was thriving. The echoes of the past were still there, a subtle hum beneath the surface, but they no longer defined her. She had found her voice, her purpose, her community. She was an artist, a teacher, a friend, a daughter, a woman who had learned to embrace the messy, imperfect tapestry of her life and create something beautiful from the broken pieces.

One evening, as she was walking home from the community center, the sky ablaze with a vibrant sunset, she realized something profound. She was happy. Not the fleeting, superficial kind of happiness, but a deep, enduring joy that resonated from within. It wasn't an absence of pain, but a presence of peace, a quiet acceptance of the past, and a hopeful embrace of the future.

She stopped and looked up at the sky, the colors mirroring the vibrant hues of her paintings. She thought of Kayla, of the sunflower, of the journey she had taken. She felt a wave of gratitude, a deep appreciation for the life she had been given, for the opportunities that lay ahead, for the connections that sustained her.

She smiled, a genuine smile that reached her eyes. She was still learning, still growing, still healing. But she was no longer afraid. She had found her light, and she was shining brightly, illuminating the world with her art, her resilience, and her unwavering hope. The seeds, scattered long ago, had not only taken root, but had blossomed into a garden, vibrant and full of life, a testament to the enduring power of the human spirit. And she, the gardener, continued to tend to it, with love, care, and an unwavering belief in the beauty that could emerge from even the darkest of soil.

The scent of oil paints and brewing coffee mingled in Imani's small apartment, a comforting aroma that had become synonymous with her mornings. Sunlight streamed through the window, illuminating the canvases that lined the walls, a vibrant testament to her ongoing journey. The gallery showing had been a turning point, a catalyst that had propelled her forward, not just as an artist, but as a person.

She took a sip of her coffee, her gaze falling on a small, framed photograph on her desk. It was a picture of her and Kayla, taken during their high school graduation, their faces beaming with youthful exuberance. A pang of sadness, a familiar ache, resonated in her chest. But it was different now. It wasn't the crushing weight of grief that had once threatened to consume her; it was a gentle reminder of a love that transcended time and loss.

A soft knock on the door interrupted her thoughts. It was Amelia, her student and friend, her face glowing with a nervous excitement. "Ready for the workshop?" she asked, her voice slightly trembling.

Today was another milestone. Imani, along with Amelia, was leading a workshop at a local community center, focused on art as a tool for healing and emotional expression. It was a collaboration with Dr. Lewis, an effort to bring the therapeutic power of art to a wider audience, particularly those struggling with grief and trauma.

Imani smiled, her heart filled with a sense of purpose. "Ready as I'll ever be," she said, her voice confident and reassuring.

The workshop was held in a large, airy room, filled with natural light. Tables were arranged with art supplies: paints, brushes, canvases, clay, and other materials. Participants, a diverse group of all ages and backgrounds, trickled in, their faces a mixture of curiosity and apprehension.

Dr. Lewis started with a brief introduction, explaining the science behind art therapy, the way creative expression could bypass the logical mind and tap into the deeper emotions. Then, Imani and Amelia took over, sharing their personal stories, their journeys of healing through art.

Imani spoke about Kayla, about the accident, about the crushing weight of grief that had threatened to suffocate her. She spoke about the fear, the anxiety, the phantom metallic tang that had haunted her for years. And then, she spoke about the art. About the way painting had become a lifeline, a way to express the emotions that words couldn't capture, a way to connect with others, a way to find meaning and purpose in the midst of her pain.

Amelia shared her story, her voice trembling slightly at first, but growing stronger with each word. She spoke about her brother, about the devastating impact of his suicide, about the guilt, the anger, the overwhelming sense of loss. She spoke about the darkness that had enveloped her, the self-harm that had become a desperate attempt to feel something, anything. And then, she spoke about the art. About the way Imani had reached out to her, about the way painting had become a safe space, a way to channel her emotions, a way to find beauty and hope in the midst of her grief.

As they spoke, Imani watched the faces of the participants. She saw tears, nods of understanding, expressions of shared pain and tentative hope. She saw the power of vulnerability, the way sharing their stories had created a sense of connection, a safe space for others to explore their own emotions.

The workshop itself was a beautiful tapestry of shared creativity and emotional expression. Participants were encouraged to choose the medium that resonated with them, to let their feelings guide their hands, to create without judgment or expectation.

Some painted, their canvases filling with vibrant colors, abstract expressions of grief, anger, hope, and resilience. Others sculpted, their hands molding clay into shapes that represented their inner landscapes. Some wrote poetry, their words capturing the raw, unfiltered emotions that flowed from their hearts.

Imani and Amelia moved around the room, offering guidance, encouragement, and support. They didn't provide answers; they offered presence, understanding, and a safe space for exploration.

One young man, his face etched with a deep sadness, struggled to even pick up a brush. Imani sat beside him, her presence quiet and reassuring. "It's okay," she said softly. "There's no right or wrong way to do this. Just... breathe. And see what happens."

Slowly, hesitantly, the young man dipped his brush into a tube of blue paint, the color of tears, the color of the ocean. He made a tentative stroke on the canvas, then another, and another. As he painted, his body began to relax, his breathing becoming deeper and more even. He didn't speak, but his emotions flowed onto the canvas, a silent expression of grief and a glimmer of hope.

An older woman, her hands trembling with age and arthritis, struggled to mold the clay. Amelia gently placed her hands over the woman's, guiding her movements, helping her shape the clay into a small, delicate bird, a symbol of freedom, of soaring above the pain.

As the workshop drew to a close, the room was filled with a quiet energy, a sense of shared accomplishment and connection. The participants gathered around, sharing their creations, their stories, their emotions. There were tears, laughter, hugs, and a profound sense of gratitude.

One woman, her eyes shining with a newfound light, approached Imani. "Thank you," she said, her voice filled with emotion. "I... I haven't felt this... free... in years. I didn't know I could... express myself like this."

Another participant, a young man who had been withdrawn and silent throughout the workshop, handed Imani a small, painted canvas. It was a simple image, a single sunflower reaching towards the sky. He didn't speak, but his eyes conveyed a message of gratitude, of hope, of connection.

As Imani and Amelia packed up the supplies, Dr. Lewis approached them, her face beaming with pride. "That was... extraordinary," she said. "You created a space for healing, for connection, for transformation. You're making a real difference in people's lives."

Imani and Amelia exchanged a smile, their hearts filled with a sense of purpose and fulfillment. It wasn't just about the art; it was about the human connection, the shared vulnerability, the power of creativity to heal and transform.

Walking home that evening, the city lights twinkling around them like a million tiny stars, Imani felt a deep sense of peace. The echoes of the past were still there, a subtle hum beneath the surface, but they no longer defined her. She was an artist, a teacher, a healer, a friend, a daughter, a woman who had learned to embrace the messy, imperfect tapestry of her life and create something beautiful from the broken pieces.

She thought of Kayla, of the sunflower, of the journey she had taken. She felt a wave of gratitude, a deep appreciation for the life she had been given, for the opportunities that lay ahead, for the connections that sustained her. She was still learning, still growing, still healing, but she was no longer defined by her past, and open to the future.

## Chapter 6

# THE DREAM OF A CENTER

The success of the workshop rippled outward, creating a gentle wave of positive change in Imani's life and the lives of those she touched. Word spread about the unique blend of art and therapy she and Amelia offered, and soon, they were receiving requests for more workshops, from schools, community centers, and even a local hospital's grief counseling program.

Imani found herself balancing her time between her own art, teaching at the community center, collaborating with Ms. Vance on new gallery opportunities, and developing the workshops with Amelia and Dr. Lewis. It was a demanding schedule, but it was also incredibly fulfilling. She was no longer just surviving; she was actively shaping her life, creating a meaningful path that honored her past and embraced the future.

Her relationship with Amelia deepened, evolving from a student-mentor dynamic into a genuine friendship. They spent hours discussing art, life, and the complexities of navigating grief. Amelia's raw talent continued to blossom, her paintings becoming bolder, more expressive, her voice as an artist finding its unique resonance.

One rainy afternoon, as they were working in Imani's apartment, surrounded by canvases and the comforting scent of paint, Amelia turned to her with a thoughtful expression. "You know," she said, "you've never really talked about your future, Imani. Beyond the art, I mean. What do you want?"

The question caught Imani off guard. She'd been so focused on healing, on helping others, on honoring Kayla's memory, that she hadn't allowed herself to truly consider her own desires, her own aspirations beyond the immediate present.

She hesitated, her gaze drifting to the framed photo of her and Kayla. "I... I don't know," she admitted, her voice barely a whisper. "It's like... I was so focused on just getting through each day, on surviving, that I forgot to... to dream."

Amelia nodded, her eyes filled with understanding. "I get it," she said. "It's like... you're afraid to want too much, because you're afraid of losing it."

Her words struck a chord deep within Imani. It was true. The fear of loss, the shadow of the accident, had cast a long shadow over her life, making her hesitant to embrace joy, to reach for happiness, to plan for a future that felt uncertain.

"But you deserve to dream, Imani," Amelia continued, her voice firm and gentle. "You deserve to be happy. Kayla would want that for you."

Imani knew Amelia was right. She'd spent so long honoring Kayla's memory by focusing on the pain of her loss that she'd forgotten to honor the joy of her life, the vibrant spirit that had radiated from her like sunshine.

"So," Amelia said, a mischievous glint in her eyes, "what do you dream of, Imani? If you could have anything, what would it be?"

Imani closed her eyes, allowing herself to imagine, to reach beyond the confines of her fear. She thought of the art, of the way it had healed her, connected her to others, given her a sense of purpose. She thought of the workshops, of the way they were making a difference in people's lives. And then, a new image emerged, a vision of a space, a sanctuary, a place where art and healing could come together in a more permanent, more profound way.

She opened her eyes, a spark of excitement igniting within her. "I... I want to create a center," she said, her voice growing stronger with each word. "A place where people can come to heal through art, to find community, to express themselves without judgment. A place like... like the workshops, but... bigger. More... permanent."

Amelia's eyes widened, her face breaking into a huge grin. "That's... amazing, Imani!" she exclaimed. "That's... that's your dream!"

And it was. It was a dream that had been quietly growing within her, nurtured by her own healing journey, by her connection with others, by her unwavering belief in the power of art. It was a dream that honored Kayla's memory, not by dwelling on the past, but by creating a future filled with hope, healing, and connection.

The idea took root, blossoming into a concrete plan. Imani and Amelia started researching, brainstorming, and sketching out their vision for the center. They envisioned a space filled with natural light, with studios for painting, sculpting, and other art forms, with a gallery to showcase the work of participants, with a quiet room for reflection and meditation, with a garden where people could connect with nature.

They named it "The Sunflower Center," a tribute to Kayla and a symbol of hope and resilience.

They approached Dr. Lewis with their idea, and she was immediately supportive. She offered her expertise in grief counseling and trauma therapy, helping them develop a holistic approach that integrated art with traditional therapeutic methods.

Ms. Vance, ever the champion of Imani's work, also offered her support, providing valuable advice on fundraising, grant writing, and navigating the complexities of establishing a non-profit organization.

The journey was challenging, filled with obstacles and setbacks. There were moments of doubt, of frustration, of feeling overwhelmed by the sheer scale of their ambition. But they persevered, fueled by their shared passion, by their unwavering belief in their vision, and by the support of their growing community.

One evening, as they were working late into the night, poring over grant applications and financial projections, Imani felt a wave of exhaustion wash over her. She leaned back in her chair, her eyes closing, the familiar fear creeping in.

"What if we fail?" she whispered, her voice filled with doubt. "What if... what if it's all too much?"

Amelia reached out and gently squeezed her hand. "We won't fail, Imani," she said, her voice firm and reassuring. "We're doing this together. And even if it takes time, even if it's hard, we'll make it happen. Because it's... it's important. It's needed."

Her words, filled with such unwavering conviction, rekindled Imani's spirit. She looked at Amelia, at the young woman who had become her friend, her partner, her inspiration, and she felt a surge of gratitude. She wasn't alone. They weren't alone. They had each other, they had their community, and they had a shared dream that was bigger than their fears.

She took a deep breath, the scent of paint and hope filling her lungs. "You're right," she said, her voice stronger now. "We'll make it happen."

And they did. Slowly, painstakingly, they navigated the complexities of fundraising, grant writing, and finding the perfect location. They rallied their community, organizing events, sharing their vision, and inspiring others to join their cause.

Finally, after months of hard work, they secured a small, but charming building in a quiet neighborhood, a space filled with natural light and surrounded by a small garden. It wasn't perfect, but it was theirs. It was a blank canvas, waiting to be transformed into a sanctuary of healing and creativity.

The Sunflower Center, a dream born from grief and nurtured by hope, was finally becoming a reality. And Imani, the girl who had once been shattered by loss, was standing at the threshold of a new chapter, her heart filled with a quiet, enduring joy, her spirit soaring, her light shining brighter than ever before. The seeds, scattered long ago, had not only taken root and blossomed, but were now spreading, carried by the wind, promising new growth, new hope, and new beginnings, wherever they landed.

# Chapter 7

# GRAND OPENING

The grand opening of The Sunflower Center was a day bathed in sunshine, a fitting tribute to its namesake and the spirit it embodied. The once-empty building buzzed with life, its walls adorned with artwork created by Imani, Amelia, and their growing community of students. The scent of fresh paint mingled with the aroma of homemade cookies, courtesy of Sarah (the classmate), creating a welcoming atmosphere that felt both vibrant and serene.

Imani stood near the entrance, her heart overflowing with a mixture of gratitude, pride, and a touch of disbelief. It was hard to believe that this space, once just a fragile dream, had blossomed into a tangible reality. She watched as visitors streamed in, their faces reflecting a range of emotions: curiosity, hope, and a quiet sense of anticipation.

Chloe, her hair a vibrant kaleidoscope of colors, flitted around, greeting guests with her infectious enthusiasm. Mr. Henderson, looking distinguished in a bow tie, offered quiet words of encouragement to the nervous artists showcasing their work. Dr. Lewis, her presence radiating a calm authority, engaged in conversations with visitors, explaining the therapeutic benefits of art.

Amelia stood beside Imani, her hand resting lightly on Imani's arm. "We did it," she whispered, her voice filled with emotion. "We actually did it."

Imani smiled, her eyes meeting Amelia's. "We did," she echoed, her voice thick with gratitude. "Together."

The opening ceremony was a simple, heartfelt affair. Imani spoke about her journey, about Kayla, about the power of art to heal and connect. She spoke about the vision of The Sunflower Center, a space where people could find solace, express their emotions, and discover their own resilience.

Amelia shared her story, her voice strong and clear, her words resonating with authenticity and vulnerability. She spoke about the darkness she had experienced, the way art had become a lifeline, and the transformative power of community.

Dr. Lewis spoke about the science behind art therapy, the way creative expression could unlock emotions, facilitate healing, and promote mental well-being.

Then, they cut the ribbon, a symbolic gesture that marked the official opening of The Sunflower Center. The crowd cheered, their applause echoing through the rooms, a wave of positive energy that filled the space with hope.

The day unfolded in a blur of conversations, connections, and shared experiences. Imani watched as people explored the studios, admired the artwork, and engaged in conversations with the artists. She saw tears, laughter, and a quiet sense of understanding passing between strangers.

A young mother, her eyes filled with a familiar sadness, approached Imani. "My son... he's been struggling since his father died," she said, her voice trembling. "I... I don't know how to help him. I heard about this place... and I thought..."

Imani gently placed her hand on the woman's arm. "We're here," she said softly. "We'll help you both. Art can be... a powerful tool."

An older gentleman, his hands gnarled with arthritis, lingered in front of a display of pottery. "I used to... I used to be a potter," he said, his voice wistful. "But... my hands... I can't..."

Amelia approached him, her smile warm and encouraging. "We have adaptive tools," she said. "We can help you find a way to... to reconnect with your passion."

Throughout the day, Imani witnessed countless moments of connection, of healing, of hope. It was a testament to the power of art, the importance of community, and the enduring resilience of the human spirit.

As the day drew to a close, and the last of the visitors departed, Imani and Amelia stood in the center of the main room, surrounded by the remnants of a beautiful day. The space was filled with a quiet energy, a sense of accomplishment, and a profound sense of gratitude.

"It's... even better than I imagined," Amelia said, her voice filled with awe.

Imani nodded, her heart overflowing. "It is," she agreed. "It's... a dream come true."

They cleaned up together, their movements synchronized by a shared sense of purpose. As they were locking up, Imani turned to Amelia, a thoughtful expression on her face.

"You know," she said, "this is just the beginning. There's so much more we can do. So many more people we can reach."

Amelia smiled, her eyes shining with excitement. "I know," she said. "And we will. Together."

They walked out into the evening air, the city lights twinkling around them like a million tiny stars. The Sunflower Center, bathed in the soft glow of the streetlights, stood as a beacon of hope, a testament to the power of healing, and a tribute to the enduring legacy of a friendship that had blossomed in the midst of grief.

Imani took a deep breath, the cool air filling her lungs. The echoes of the past were still there, a subtle hum beneath the surface, but they no longer defined her. She was an artist, a healer, a friend, a daughter, a woman who had transformed her pain into purpose, her grief into growth, her loss into love.

She looked at Amelia, her friend, her partner, her inspiration, and she felt a surge of gratitude. They had created something beautiful, something meaningful, something that would touch countless lives.

And as they walked away, hand in hand, towards the future, Imani knew that the journey ahead would be filled with challenges, with setbacks, with moments of doubt. But she also knew that they would face them together, with courage, with resilience, and with an unwavering belief in the power of art to heal the world, one brushstroke, one sculpture, one story at a time. The sunflower, a symbol of hope and resilience, had not only bloomed in their hearts, but had seeded a garden, a sanctuary, a testament to the enduring power of the human spirit to overcome even the darkest of nights. And the garden, tended with love and care, would continue to grow, to flourish, and to spread its light to all who sought its solace.

# Chapter 8

# KAYLA'S JOURNAL

The following months were a whirlwind of activity, growth, and the quiet satisfaction of witnessing The Sunflower Center blossom into the haven they had envisioned. Word of mouth spread like wildfire, fueled by the positive experiences of those who found solace and healing within its walls. They quickly outgrew the initial schedule of classes, adding workshops on art journaling, trauma-informed yoga, and even a support group for bereaved parents, facilitated by Dr. Lewis.

Imani found herself juggling multiple roles – administrator, artist, teacher, and sometimes, just a listening ear. She thrived on the energy, the constant interaction with people seeking connection and expression. But she also recognized the need to pace herself, to avoid the burnout that could easily creep in when passion projects became all-consuming.

One crisp autumn afternoon, while Imani was organizing art supplies in the storage room, her phone buzzed. It was a text from her mother: "Dinner at our place Sunday? Maya's making your favorite – lasagna!" A wave of warmth washed over Imani. Family dinners had become a cherished ritual, a grounding constant amidst the ever-shifting landscape of her life.

"Sounds perfect! See you then," she texted back.

As she put her phone away, she noticed a small, unopened box tucked away on a shelf. It was labeled "Kayla's Things," in her mother's handwriting. Imani had avoided opening it for years, the memories it held too painful to confront. But today, something shifted. A quiet curiosity, a gentle nudge from within, prompted her to reach for it.

She carried the box to her small office, a cozy space filled with her artwork and the comforting scent of paint. Sitting at her desk, she hesitated for a moment, then carefully opened the box. Inside were mementos of their friendship: photographs, letters, dried flowers, a mix-tape labeled "Road Trip Anthems," a chipped ceramic sunflower that Kayla had made in a pottery class.

Each object evoked a flood of memories, a bittersweet ache in her chest. She saw their smiling faces in the photographs, heard Kayla's infectious laughter in her mind, felt the phantom touch of their friendship. Tears welled up in her eyes, but they weren't the tears of crushing grief that had once consumed her. They were tears of remembrance, of love, of gratitude for the bond they had shared.

As she sifted through the contents of the box, she found a small, leather-bound journal. It was Kayla's. Imani had never seen it before. Her heart pounded in her chest as she opened it, her fingers tracing the familiar handwriting on the cover.

The journal entries were a window into Kayla's inner world, a glimpse of her thoughts, her dreams, her vulnerabilities. Imani read about Kayla's passion for art, her aspirations to become a photographer, her anxieties about the future, her unwavering love for her family and friends.

And then, she found an entry dated a few weeks before the accident.

"I had a dream last night," Kayla had written. "I was standing in a field of sunflowers, their faces turned towards the sun. And Imani was there, painting. She was surrounded by people, all different ages, all different backgrounds. And they were all creating, all healing. It was... beautiful. I woke up feeling... hopeful. Like... like we could make a difference in the world, somehow."

Imani's breath caught in her throat. Kayla's dream, so eerily similar to the vision of The Sunflower Center, felt like a message from beyond, a validation of their journey, a confirmation that they were on the right path.

Tears streamed down her face, a mixture of grief, joy, and a profound sense of connection. She closed the journal, holding it close to her heart. It was a reminder of Kayla's enduring spirit, of the power of dreams, and of the unwavering bond that continued to inspire her.

That evening, as she was preparing for bed, Amelia called. "Hey," she said, her voice bubbling with excitement. "Guess what? We got the grant! The big one! The one for expanding the center!"

Imani's heart leaped. The grant was a game-changer. It would allow them to renovate the building, add more studios, create a dedicated gallery space, and hire additional staff. It was a validation of their work, a recognition of the impact they were making in the community.

"That's... incredible, Amelia!" Imani exclaimed, her voice filled with disbelief and joy. "That's... that's amazing!"

They talked for a long time, their voices filled with excitement and plans for the future. The Sunflower Center was growing, evolving, reaching more people than they had ever imagined.

As Imani hung up the phone, she felt a surge of gratitude. She looked at the small, ceramic sunflower on her desk, a memento from Kayla's box, a symbol of hope and resilience. She thought of Kayla's dream, of the field of sunflowers, of the people creating and healing.

She smiled, a genuine smile that reached her eyes. They were making a difference. They were honoring Kayla's memory, not just by remembering her, but by living her dream, by creating a space where others could find solace, express their emotions, and discover their own resilience. The sunflower, once a symbol of loss, had become a symbol of hope, of growth, of a future filled with light and possibility. And Imani, the girl who had once been shattered by grief, was now tending to that garden, nurturing its growth, and sharing its beauty with the world.

The next day, Imani shared Kayla's journal entry with Amelia. They were silent for a while, sitting on the floor of Imani's office, surrounded by all of Imani's art. The journal was open on the floor between them.

"It's like... she knew," Amelia finally said, her voice hushed.

Imani nodded. "It feels that way."

"So, what do we do with this information?"

Imani thought for a moment. "We keep going. We build the center that Kayla dreamed of. We make it even better than we imagined."

Amelia met Imani's eyes. "Together."

Imani smiled. "Together."

# Chapter 9

# EXPANDING THE VISION

T he expansion of The Sunflower Center was a symphony of organized chaos. Construction crews swarmed the building, their hammers and drills a constant counterpoint to the quiet hum of creativity that still permeated the existing studios. Dust motes danced in the sunbeams that streamed through the newly enlarged windows, illuminating the progress that was transforming the once-small space into a true sanctuary.

Imani and Amelia navigated the construction zone with a practiced ease, their days filled with meetings with architects, contractors, and potential donors. They were learning on the fly, mastering the intricacies of building codes, fundraising strategies, and the delicate art of balancing their artistic vision with the practical realities of construction.

Dr. Lewis, ever the grounding force, helped them create a temporary schedule, moving classes to different locations, utilizing outdoor spaces when the weather permitted, and maintaining a sense of continuity amidst the disruption. The community rallied around them, volunteers offering their time and skills, local businesses donating materials, and participants patiently adapting to the changing environment.

One afternoon, as Imani and Amelia were reviewing blueprints in the makeshift office they had set up in the garden shed, a young man approached them. He was tall and lanky, with a hesitant smile and kind eyes. He introduced himself as Leo, a landscape architect.

"I heard about The Sunflower Center," he said, "and I was... inspired. I'd love to offer my services, pro bono, to design the garden. I envision a space that's both beautiful and therapeutic, a place where people can connect with nature and find peace."

Imani and Amelia exchanged a surprised and delighted glance. It was a serendipitous moment, a perfect example of the way the community was embracing their vision and contributing their unique talents.

"That's... amazing, Leo," Imani said, her voice filled with gratitude. "We'd love that. We've always envisioned the garden as an integral part of the center."

Leo's design was a masterpiece of mindful landscaping. He incorporated winding paths, secluded seating areas, a small pond with a gentle waterfall, and a vibrant array of plants chosen for their sensory qualities – fragrant herbs, colorful flowers, and textured foliage. He even included a "sensory garden" specifically designed for children and individuals with sensory processing differences.

As the construction progressed, the center began to take shape. The new studios were spacious and light-filled, equipped with state-of-the-art equipment. The gallery space was elegant and inviting, designed to showcase the work of both established and emerging artists. The quiet room, painted in soothing shades of blue and green, offered a tranquil retreat for meditation and reflection.

One evening, as Imani and Amelia were walking through the nearly completed building, they stopped in the new gallery space. Sunlight streamed through the large windows, illuminating the empty walls, waiting to be filled with art.

"It's... breathtaking," Amelia whispered, her voice filled with awe.

Imani nodded, her heart overflowing with emotion. "It is," she agreed. "It's... everything we dreamed of, and more."

They stood in silence for a moment, absorbing the energy of the space, the culmination of their hard work, their shared vision, and the unwavering support of their community. It was a testament to the power of dreams, the resilience of the human spirit, and the transformative potential of art.

"Kayla would have loved this," Amelia said softly, her eyes glistening with tears.

Imani reached out and gently squeezed her hand. "She would," she agreed, her voice thick with emotion. "She's here, Amelia. In every brushstroke, in every sculpture, in every heart that finds healing here. She's here."

The grand re-opening of The Sunflower Center was an even bigger celebration than the first. The expanded space buzzed with excitement, filled with artists, students, community members, and even a few local dignitaries. The walls were adorned with vibrant artwork, the air filled with the sounds of laughter, conversation, and the gentle strains of live music.

Imani and Amelia, standing side by side, greeted guests with radiant smiles, their hearts overflowing with gratitude and pride. They had created something truly special, a sanctuary of healing, a testament to the power of art, and a lasting tribute to the enduring legacy of a friendship that had blossomed in the midst of grief.

As Imani looked around the room, at the faces of the people whose lives had been touched by The Sunflower Center, she felt a profound sense of peace. The echoes of the past were still there, a subtle hum beneath the surface, but they no longer defined her. She had found her purpose, her community, her voice. She was an artist, a healer, a leader, a friend, a daughter, a woman who had transformed her pain into a beacon of hope, illuminating the world with her art, her resilience, and her unwavering belief in the power of the human spirit to overcome even the darkest of nights.

The sunflower, once a symbol of loss, had become a symbol of growth, of transformation, of a future filled with endless possibilities. And Imani, the gardener of that vibrant, ever-expanding garden, continued to tend to it with love, care, and an unwavering commitment to sharing its beauty with the world. The seeds, scattered long ago, had not only taken root and blossomed, but were now being carried by the wind, spreading hope, healing, and connection far beyond the walls of The Sunflower Center, promising new growth, new beginnings, and a future where art could truly change the world, one heart at a time. The legacy of the ceramic sunflower was secure.

The Sunflower Center, now expanded and buzzing with a vibrant energy, continued to evolve, not just as a physical space, but as a living, breathing entity. It became a hub for the community, a place where people from all walks of life converged to explore their creativity, find solace, and connect with others.

One initiative that blossomed organically was the "Art in the Park" program. Every Saturday, weather permitting, a group of volunteers, led by Amelia, would set up easels, paints, and other art supplies in a nearby park. It was an open invitation to anyone who wanted to create, regardless of skill level or experience. Children, seniors, families, and even a few curious dogs found themselves drawn to the vibrant scene, their faces lighting up with the simple joy of expressing themselves.

Imani, while often busy with the administrative aspects of the center, made it a point to join the park sessions whenever she could. There was something incredibly grounding about creating art outdoors, surrounded by the sounds of nature and the laughter of children. She found herself connecting with people she might never have met otherwise, sharing stories, offering encouragement, and witnessing the transformative power of art in its most accessible form.

One Saturday, a young boy, no older than seven, approached Imani with a hesitant smile. He was clutching a crumpled piece

of paper, a drawing of a single, wilting sunflower. "My grandma...
she died," he whispered, his voice barely audible. "She... she loved
sunflowers."

Imani's heart ached for the boy, recognizing the familiar pang
of loss. She knelt beside him, her voice gentle. "I'm so sorry," she
said. "It's... the hardest thing. But you know what? Sunflowers...
they're strong. Even when they wilt, they leave behind seeds. Seeds
that can grow into new sunflowers. And your grandma... she left
behind seeds, too. Seeds of love, of memories, of all the things that
made her special. And those seeds... they'll always be with you."

She helped the boy find a fresh canvas and some paints. Together, they painted a vibrant field of sunflowers, their golden heads
reaching towards the sky. As they painted, the boy's sadness began
to lift, replaced by a quiet sense of peace. He was connecting with
his grief, expressing his emotions, and finding a way to honor his
grandmother's memory.

That evening, as Imani was walking home, she received a text
from Amelia: "Another amazing day in the park! So many smiles,
so much creativity. We're making a difference, Imani. We really
are."

Imani smiled, her heart filled with gratitude. The Sunflower
Center, born from a dream of healing and connection, was rip-
pling outward, touching lives in ways she had never imagined.

As the center continued to thrive, Imani found herself facing
a new challenge: balancing her own artistic aspirations with the
demands of running a growing organization. She loved teaching,
loved connecting with the community, but she also yearned to

return to her own studio, to lose herself in the creative process, to express the emotions that still swirled within her.

Ms. Vance, ever the perceptive mentor, noticed Imani's quiet struggle. "You need to nurture your own art, Imani," she said one afternoon, as they were discussing upcoming gallery opportunities. "You can't pour from an empty cup. The center is thriving, but you need to make time for yourself, for your own creative voice."

Her words resonated deeply with Imani. She knew Ms. Vance was right. She had been so focused on building The Sunflower Center, on helping others, that she had neglected her own artistic needs.

She decided to carve out dedicated time each week for her own studio practice. It wasn't easy. There were always emails to answer, meetings to attend, and unexpected crises to manage. But she made it a priority, treating her studio time as sacred, a non-negotiable commitment to her own well-being.

She started a new series of paintings, exploring the theme of resilience, not just in the context of grief, but in the broader spectrum of human experience. She painted portraits of the people she had met at the center, capturing their strength, their vulnerability, their unique journeys of healing. She painted landscapes, inspired by the beauty of the natural world, the way it constantly renewed itself, even after the harshest of winters.

One evening, as she was working on a large canvas, depicting a field of wildflowers emerging from a cracked and barren landscape, she felt a familiar presence beside her. It wasn't a physical presence, but a feeling, a sense of connection, a whisper of encouragement.

She thought of Kayla, of the ceramic sunflower, of the dream journal entry. She felt a wave of gratitude, a deep appreciation for the journey she had taken, for the challenges she had overcome, for the life she was creating.

She smiled, a genuine smile that radiated from within. She was still learning, still growing, still healing. But she was no longer afraid. She had found her voice, her purpose, her community. And she was using her art, not just to heal herself, but to illuminate the world, one brushstroke at a time. The garden, planted long ago, was not only thriving, but inspiring new growth, new hope, and new beginnings, wherever its seeds were scattered. And she, the gardener, continued to tend to it, with love, care, and an unwavering belief in the power of beauty to transform even the most desolate of landscapes.

# Chapter 10

# RESILIENCE THROUGH SHARED STORIES

The Sunflower Center's reputation continued to grow, attracting not only individuals seeking solace and healing, but also artists and therapists interested in collaborating. It became a vibrant hub, a testament to the ripple effect of compassion and creativity. One such collaboration led to an unexpected opportunity, one that would challenge Imani and stretch her artistic boundaries in ways she hadn't anticipated.

A renowned art therapist, Dr. Anya Sharma, who specialized in working with veterans suffering from PTSD, reached out to Imani. Dr. Sharma had been following The Sunflower Center's progress with great interest and proposed a joint project: a series of workshops culminating in a public art installation, created collaboratively by veterans and members of the community. The theme: "Resilience Through Shared Stories."

Imani was both excited and intimidated. While she had experience working with individuals navigating grief and trauma, the specific challenges faced by veterans felt like a different landscape. She knew the power of art to heal, but she also recognized the importance of approaching this project with sensitivity, respect, and a deep understanding of the unique experiences of those who had served in the military.

She and Amelia met with Dr. Sharma to discuss the logistics. The workshops would be held at The Sunflower Center, utilizing the expanded facilities and the tranquil garden space designed by Leo. Dr. Sharma would lead the therapeutic aspects, guiding the veterans through their emotional journeys, while Imani and Amelia would facilitate the artistic expression, helping participants translate their experiences into visual narratives.

"The key," Dr. Sharma emphasized, "is to create a safe and supportive environment. Many veterans struggle with feelings of isolation, of not being understood. The art will be a bridge, a way to connect with others, to share their stories without having to rely solely on words."

Imani took Dr. Sharma's words to heart. She spent hours researching, reading accounts of veterans' experiences, and familiarizing herself with the specific challenges of PTSD, moral injury, and the difficult transition back to civilian life. She wanted to be prepared, not just as an artist, but as a compassionate listener and facilitator.

The first workshop was filled with a palpable tension. The veterans, a diverse group representing different branches of service and eras of conflict, were hesitant, their faces guarded, their eyes reflecting a mixture of apprehension and quiet hope. The community members, a mix of artists and individuals who had simply been drawn to the project, were equally unsure, their empathy tempered by a sense of respectful distance.

Dr. Sharma began by creating a circle, a space for sharing and connection. She spoke about the power of storytelling, the way it could help to process trauma, build bridges, and foster understanding. She then invited each participant to introduce themselves, not by their rank or military experience, but by sharing something they loved, something that brought them joy.

The ice began to thaw. A gruff-looking sergeant spoke about his love for woodworking, the way the feel of the wood in his hands calmed his anxieties. A young woman, her eyes filled with a quiet sadness, shared her passion for gardening, the way nurturing plants helped her to feel grounded. A retired officer spoke about his love for music, the way playing the guitar helped him to express emotions he couldn't articulate in words.

As the veterans shared their stories, Imani and Amelia began to sketch, capturing the essence of their words in visual form. They weren't creating portraits, but rather abstract representations of their emotions, their struggles, and their resilience. The act of drawing, of translating their experiences into lines and colors, became a shared language, a bridge between the veterans and the community members.

Over the following weeks, the workshops evolved into a powerful tapestry of shared creativity and emotional exploration. The veterans, initially hesitant, began to open up, their stories unfolding in layers of paint, clay, and mixed media. They spoke of their experiences in combat, the trauma they had witnessed, the losses they had endured, and the challenges they faced in readjusting to civilian life.

The community members listened, their hearts filled with empathy and respect. They offered their support, not as experts, but as fellow human beings, willing to bear witness to the pain and resilience of those who had served.

The art became a conduit, a way to express the unspeakable, to connect with others, and to find a sense of shared humanity. The canvases filled with images of war and peace, of loss and hope, of brokenness and healing. The sculptures took shape, representing the weight of trauma, the strength of the human spirit, and the enduring power of connection.

One veteran, a quiet man named Michael, who had initially been reluctant to participate, found himself drawn to the clay. He spent hours shaping and reshaping the material, his hands working intuitively, his emotions flowing into the form. He created a series of small, fragile figures, representing the men and women he had served with, those who had survived and those who had not.

"It's... it's like I'm giving them a voice," he said, his voice trembling slightly. "A way to... to remember them. To honor them."

Another veteran, a young woman named Sarah, who had struggled with severe PTSD and feelings of isolation, found solace in painting. She created large, abstract canvases, filled with vibrant colors and swirling patterns. "It's like... I'm letting go of the darkness," she said. "And finding... a new light."

As the workshops progressed, Imani found herself deeply moved by the stories she was witnessing, the courage of the veterans, and the unwavering support of the community members. She realized that the art wasn't just about healing; it was about building bridges, fostering understanding, and creating a space for shared humanity.

The final art installation, displayed in the expanded gallery space of The Sunflower Center, was a powerful testament to the journey they had all taken together. It was a tapestry of interwoven stories, a visual representation of resilience, healing, and the enduring power of the human spirit.

The opening reception was a moving event, attended by veterans, community members, local dignitaries, and even a few representatives from the Department of Veterans Affairs. The atmosphere was charged with emotion, a mixture of pride, gratitude, and a quiet sense of accomplishment.

As Imani stood beside Amelia, watching the visitors interact with the artwork, she felt a profound sense of peace. The Sunflower Center, born from a dream of healing and connection, had blossomed into something far greater than she had ever imagined. It was a living testament to the power of art, the resilience of the human spirit, and the enduring legacy of a friendship that had transcended loss and inspired a community to come together, to heal, to grow, and to create a world where even the deepest wounds could find a path to healing and hope. The ceramic sunflower, a small memento of a friendship, had become a symbol, a beacon, illuminating the way for countless others to find their own light.

## Chapter 11

# GROWING PAINS

The success of "Resilience Through Shared Stories" reverberated far beyond the walls of The Sunflower Center. News outlets picked up the story, showcasing the powerful artwork and the moving testimonials of the veterans. Invitations poured in for Imani, Amelia, and Dr. Sharma to present their collaborative model at conferences and workshops across the country. The Sunflower Center became a nationally recognized model for integrating art and therapy, a beacon of hope for communities seeking innovative ways to address trauma and foster healing.

For Imani, the whirlwind of attention was both exhilarating and humbling. She found herself navigating a new landscape of public speaking, media interviews, and strategic partnerships. It was a far cry from the quiet solitude of her studio, but she embraced the opportunity to share the message of The Sunflower Center, to advocate for the power of art to transform lives.

One unexpected consequence of the increased visibility was a flood of requests for individual therapy and art classes. The waiting list grew exponentially, stretching the center's resources to their limit. Imani, Amelia, and Dr. Lewis found themselves working longer hours, juggling administrative tasks with their commitment to providing direct care.

One evening, after a particularly long day, Imani and Amelia sat in the garden, the soft glow of the setting sun casting long shadows across the tranquil space. The sounds of the city were muted, replaced by the gentle rustling of leaves and the chirping of crickets.

"We need help," Amelia said, her voice laced with exhaustion. "We can't keep up with this demand."

Imani nodded, her own fatigue mirroring Amelia's. "I know," she said. "But we also need to be careful. We don't want to compromise the quality of what we offer. The Sunflower Center is special because it's... intimate. It's a community, not just a clinic."

They brainstormed ideas, exploring options for expanding their team, training new facilitators, and developing online resources to reach a wider audience. They were committed to maintaining the core values of The Sunflower Center – compassion, connection, and a deep respect for the individual journey – while also adapting to the growing needs of the community.

One solution emerged organically. Several of the participants from the veterans' workshops, having experienced the transformative power of art firsthand, expressed a desire to become facilitators themselves. They had walked the path of healing, and now they wanted to help others do the same.

Imani and Amelia, with Dr. Sharma's guidance, developed a comprehensive training program, designed to equip these individuals with the skills and knowledge necessary to lead art-based support groups. It was a rigorous curriculum, covering topics such as trauma-informed care, group dynamics, and ethical considerations. But it was also deeply rooted in the experiential learning that had become the hallmark of The Sunflower Center.

The first cohort of trainees included Michael, the quiet veteran who had found solace in sculpting, and Sarah, the young woman who had used painting to express her journey through PTSD. They brought a unique perspective to the training, their lived experiences adding a layer of authenticity and empathy that resonated deeply with the other trainees.

As Imani watched these individuals blossom into confident and compassionate facilitators, she felt a profound sense of pride. The Sunflower Center was not only healing individuals; it was empowering them to become agents of healing in their own communities. It was a ripple effect, a testament to the enduring power of human connection and the transformative potential of art.

Another significant development was the establishment of a scholarship fund, designed to make The Sunflower Center's programs accessible to individuals who couldn't afford the fees. The fund was supported by donations from individuals, foundations, and local businesses, all inspired by the center's mission and the stories of healing that emerged from its walls.

One evening, Imani received a handwritten letter from a young woman who had benefited from the scholarship fund. "The Sunflower Center saved my life," she wrote. "I was lost, broken, and drowning in grief after losing my brother to suicide. The art... it gave me a voice. It helped me to express the emotions I couldn't put into words. And the community... it gave me a sense of belonging, a feeling that I wasn't alone. Thank you... for giving me hope again."

Tears welled up in Imani's eyes as she read the letter. It was a powerful reminder of the impact The Sunflower Center was having, the lives it was touching, the hope it was fostering. It was a validation of their journey, a confirmation that their dream, born from grief and nurtured by love, was making a real difference in the world.

As the center continued to grow and evolve, Imani found herself reflecting on her own journey. She was no longer the shattered girl who had sought refuge in a chipped ceramic mug and the quiet solitude of her apartment. She was a leader, an artist, a healer, a woman who had transformed her pain into purpose.

She still carried the echoes of the past, the memory of Kayla, the phantom metallic tang that sometimes surfaced during moments of stress. But they no longer defined her. They were a part of her story, a reminder of the resilience she had discovered within herself, the strength she had found in connection, and the transformative power of art.

One sunny afternoon, Imani found herself back in her own studio, a space she had neglected for too long. She stood before a blank canvas, a palette of vibrant colors at her side. She closed her eyes, took a deep breath, and allowed herself to connect with the emotions that swirled within her.

She began to paint, not with a specific image in mind, but with a sense of freedom, of exploration, of allowing her intuition to guide her hand. Colors flowed onto the canvas, blending and swirling, creating a tapestry of light and shadow, of joy and sorrow, of grief and hope.

As she painted, she felt a sense of peace, a quiet connection to her own creative spirit. She was home. She was whole. She was an artist, a healer, a woman who had found her voice, her purpose, and her light. And she was shining brightly, illuminating the world with her art, her compassion, and her unwavering belief in the power of the human spirit to overcome even the darkest of nights. The garden, planted long ago, continued to flourish, its seeds spreading far and wide, promising new growth, new beginnings, and a future where art could truly heal the world, one heart, one brushstroke, at a time. The legacy of a single ceramic sunflower, and the girl who'd made it, lived on.

# Chapter 12

# TEN YEARS

The tenth anniversary of The Sunflower Center arrived, not with a grand, formal celebration, but with a week-long series of events, each reflecting the heart of what they had built. There were open studio sessions, where visitors could wander through the spaces and witness the creative process firsthand. There were collaborative art projects, inviting everyone to contribute to large-scale murals and sculptures. There were storytelling circles, where individuals shared their journeys of healing and resilience. And there was, of course, a garden party, held in the space that Leo had so beautifully designed, filled with music, laughter, and the shared joy of a community that had blossomed from the seeds of grief.

Imani found herself moving through the week with a sense of quiet wonder. It was hard to believe that a decade had passed since she and Amelia had first sketched out their dream on a scrap of paper in her small apartment. So much had changed, yet the core essence of The Sunflower Center remained the same: a sanctuary of healing, a testament to the power of art, and a tribute to the enduring legacy of a friendship that had transcended loss.

One evening, as the sun began to set, casting a golden glow over the garden, Imani found herself alone, sitting on a bench near the small pond that Leo had created. The sounds of the city were muted, replaced by the gentle murmur of the waterfall and the chirping of crickets. She closed her eyes, taking a deep breath, allowing herself to simply be present in the moment.

She thought of Kayla, of the chipped ceramic sunflower, of the dream journal entry that had felt like a message from beyond. She felt a wave of gratitude, a deep appreciation for the journey she had taken, for the challenges she had overcome, for the life she had created.

She thought of Amelia, her friend, her partner, her inspiration. Their bond, forged in the crucible of grief and nurtured by shared purpose, had become one of the most important relationships in her life. They had supported each other, challenged each other, and celebrated each other's triumphs, creating a partnership that was both strong and deeply fulfilling.

She thought of Dr. Lewis, her therapist, her mentor, her friend. Her gentle guidance, her unwavering support, and her belief in Imani's strength had been instrumental in her healing journey.

She thought of Ms. Vance, the gallery owner who had taken a chance on a grieving young artist and had become a champion of her work. Her encouragement, her business acumen, and her belief in Imani's talent had opened doors she had never dreamed possible.

She thought of Leo, the landscape architect who had transformed the garden into a therapeutic oasis, his vision and talent adding another layer of beauty and healing to The Sunflower Center.

She thought of Michael and Sarah, the veterans who had found solace in art and had become facilitators, sharing their experiences and empowering others to find their own paths to healing.

She thought of all the individuals who had walked through the doors of The Sunflower Center, seeking solace, expression, and connection. Their stories, their struggles, their resilience, had touched her deeply, shaping her understanding of the human condition and reinforcing her belief in the power of art to heal.

As she sat there, surrounded by the beauty of the garden, she felt a profound sense of peace. The echoes of the past were still there, a subtle hum beneath the surface, but they no longer defined her. She had found her voice, her purpose, her community. She was an artist, a healer, a leader, a friend, a daughter, a woman who had transformed her pain into a beacon of hope.

A gentle touch on her arm startled her. She opened her eyes and saw Amelia standing beside her, a warm smile on her face.

"Penny for your thoughts?" Amelia asked softly.

Imani smiled. "Just... reflecting," she said. "Thinking about how far we've come."

Amelia sat down beside her, their shoulders touching. "It's... incredible, isn't it?" she said. "Sometimes I still can't believe it's real."

"Me neither," Imani agreed. "But it is. We did it. Together."

They sat in silence for a moment, their shared history a palpable presence between them. Then, Amelia turned to Imani, her eyes filled with a mischievous glint.

"So," she said, "what's next?"

Imani laughed, a genuine, joyful sound that echoed through the garden. "What do you mean?" she asked.

"I mean," Amelia said, "we've built this amazing center. We've helped so many people. But... what's the next dream? What's the next mountain we're going to climb?"

Imani thought for a moment, her gaze drifting across the garden, the faces of the sunflowers, now illuminated by the soft glow of lanterns that had been lit as darkness fell. A new idea, a seed of possibility, began to germinate within her.

"I've been thinking," she said, her voice filled with a growing excitement. "About... expanding our reach. About taking the model of The Sunflower Center... and sharing it with other communities. About creating... a network. A network of Sunflower Centers, all across the country, all across the world."

Amelia's eyes widened, her face breaking into a huge grin. "That's... that's brilliant, Imani!" she exclaimed. "That's... that's our next dream!"

And it was. It was a dream that built upon the foundation they had laid, a dream that honored Kayla's memory, not just by remembering her, but by spreading her light, her spirit, her love of art, to countless others. It was a dream that would require even more hard work, more dedication, more collaboration. But it was a dream that felt right, a dream that resonated with their shared purpose, a dream that promised to bring healing, hope, and connection to even more communities.

As they sat there, in the heart of the garden that had become a symbol of their journey, Imani knew that the road ahead would be long and winding, filled with challenges and triumphs. But she also knew that they would face it together, with courage, with resilience, and with an unwavering belief in the power of art to heal the world.

The sunflower, once a symbol of loss, had become a symbol of hope, of growth, of a future filled with endless possibilities. And Imani, the gardener of that vibrant, ever-expanding garden, was ready to plant new seeds, to nurture new growth, and to share the beauty of her creation with the world, one sunflower, one community, one heart at a time. The chipped ceramic sunflower, now resting on a shelf in Imani's office, a treasured memento of a friendship that had changed everything, was a reminder of where it all began, and a promise of the beauty that was still to come. The echoes had faded, replaced by the sounds of growth, and the future was bright, a canvas waiting to be filled.

# Chapter 13

# SPREADING SEEDS

The idea of a network of Sunflower Centers, a constellation of healing spaces spread across the map, took root quickly. It was ambitious, bordering on audacious, but it resonated with a deep, undeniable truth: the need for accessible, community-based mental health support, particularly through the arts, was vast and largely unmet.

The initial steps were daunting. They weren't simply replicating the existing center; they were creating a blueprint, a model that could be adapted and implemented in diverse communities, each with its own unique needs and resources. Imani and Amelia spent weeks brainstorming, researching existing franchise and non-profit network models, and consulting with experts in organizational development.

Dr. Lewis, as always, provided invaluable guidance. "Think of it like a dandelion," she suggested one afternoon, during a brainstorming session in the garden. "The seed head – that's your core model, the essence of The Sunflower Center. The individual seeds – those are the new centers, each slightly different, adapted to their environment, but carrying the same DNA."

The metaphor resonated deeply. It captured the essence of their vision: a network that was both unified and diverse, grounded in the same core principles but adaptable to the specific needs of each community.

They developed a comprehensive "toolkit," a guide for establishing new Sunflower Centers. It included everything from sample budgets and fundraising strategies to curriculum outlines and best practices for trauma-informed care. They also created a training program for new center directors and facilitators, emphasizing the importance of community engagement, cultural sensitivity, and the ethical considerations of providing art-based therapy.

The first expansion location was a pilot project, a test case for their model. They chose a small town in a neighboring state, a community that had been grappling with a high rate of opioid addiction and a lack of mental health resources. Imani and Amelia spent months working with local leaders, community organizers, and potential staff, laying the groundwork for the new center.

The process was challenging. There were logistical hurdles, funding challenges, and moments of doubt. But they persevered, driven by their unwavering belief in their vision and the support of their growing network.

The grand opening of the second Sunflower Center was a smaller, more intimate affair than the re-opening of the original, but it was no less significant. The local community embraced the center with open arms, grateful for the resources and support it offered. The artists who would be teaching and practicing there were passionate and ready.

As Imani watched the new center director, a young woman named Sarah (a different Sarah, this time), cut the ribbon, she felt a surge of pride and gratitude. It was a tangible manifestation of their dream, a testament to the power of collaboration, and a confirmation that their model could be replicated, bringing healing and hope to new communities.

But the expansion wasn't without its personal challenges for Imani. She found herself traveling frequently, spending days away from her own studio, from the familiar comfort of her home, and from the community she had helped to build. The constant demands of managing a growing organization, of mentoring new leaders, and of advocating for the importance of art therapy began to take a toll.

One evening, after a particularly grueling trip, Imani returned to her apartment, feeling exhausted and emotionally drained. She walked into her studio, the space that had always been her sanctuary, and felt a pang of longing. The canvases were stacked against the wall, the brushes were dry, the paints were untouched. She had been so focused on building the network that she had neglected her own creative well-being.

She sat down at her easel, her gaze falling on a blank canvas. She picked up a brush, dipped it into a vibrant shade of yellow, the color of sunflowers, the color of hope. She hesitated for a moment, then made a tentative stroke on the canvas.

It was a small gesture, a simple act of returning to her own creative source. But it was enough. As she painted, the tension in her body began to ease, the exhaustion fading, replaced by a quiet sense of peace. She was reconnecting with her own inner landscape, reminding herself that she, too, needed nurturing, that she, too, needed to tend to her own garden.

The journey of expanding The Sunflower Center network was just beginning. It would be filled with challenges, with setbacks, with moments of doubt. But Imani knew that she wasn't alone. She had Amelia, her partner, her friend, her unwavering support. She had Dr. Lewis, her mentor, her guide, her voice of wisdom. She had a growing network of passionate individuals, all committed to bringing the healing power of art to their communities.

And she had her own art, her own creative voice, her own inner sunflower, reminding her to stay grounded, to stay connected to her purpose, and to continue to bloom, even in the midst of the most demanding of seasons. The chipped ceramic sunflower, a constant reminder of where it all began, was a touchstone, a reminder that even the smallest of seeds, planted with love and intention, could grow into something extraordinary.

# ABOUT THE AUTHOR

I 've spent over four decades watching and participating in the digital revolution. From my first encounters with computer programming in high school during the late 1970s to navigating today's complex cyber landscape, technology has been a constant companion in my journey. While serving in the U.S. Army during Desert Storm, I witnessed firsthand how rapidly technology could evolve and transform our capabilities.

Now, as I navigate my senior years, I find myself in a unique position – someone who understands both the tremendous potential and the growing challenges of our digital age. This book represents not just my knowledge, but our shared experience as we continue to adapt and learn in this ever-changing digital world.

Through her writing, Rene' aims to illuminate the positive aspects of life's journey, drawing from her varied experiences to create stories that resonate with readers of all backgrounds.

Readers can discover more about Rene's work at www.books-by-rene.store